Wild About the Bible

Sticker & Activity Book

Pictures by David Miles

Copyright © 2016 by Zonderkidz

Requests for information should be addressed to:
Zonderkidz, 3900 Sparks Drive SE, Grand Rapids, Michigan 49546

ISBN 978-0-310-75405-3

Editor: Mary Hassinger
Cover Design: Cindy Davis
Interior design: Kris Nelson

Printed in China

15 16 17 18 19 20 21 /DHC/ 6 5 4 3 2 1

ZONDERkidz

God spent seven days creating his world.

On the first day, God made light.

On the second day, God made seas and oceans and sky.

On the third day, God made land. Every kind of plant was created too.

On the fourth day, the sun, moon, and stars were formed.

God made creatures that lived in the skies and seas on the fifth day.

And on the sixth day, God made animals and human beings.

Then God rested!

Find the stickers to finish the picture.

Two of every animal on earth came to Noah's ark. Help the giraffes find their way.

start

end

Solve the secret code to find the hidden Bible verse from the story of the Lost Son.

__ __　__ __ __　__ __ __ __　__ __ __　__ __　__ __ __ __ __ __ .

13　7　　21　20　9　　1　19　9　8　　20　23　25　　12　9　　24　19　17　23　25

A = 20	E = 7	I = 12	M = 26	Q = 10	U = 17	Y = 22
B = 2	F = 24	J = 6	N = 23	R = 26	V = 5	Z = 18
C = 11	G = 4	K = 15	O = 19	S = 9	W = 21	
D = 25	H = 13	L = 1	P = 3	T = 8	X = 14	

One day, Jesus and his disciples went up on a mountain. They were telling people about God.

What do you think it looked like that day? Color the picture.

Use the clues below to fill in the crossword puzzle.

Hint: read the story about Moses
and his people leaving Egypt in Exodus 7-14.

Across

2. The Israelites used this animal to protect their sons against the tenth plague.

5. The place where Pharaoh treated the Israelites as slaves.

7. The amphibians that were part of God's ten plagues.

8. Where the Israelites were going when they left Egypt.

10. What the bush Moses saw was doing.

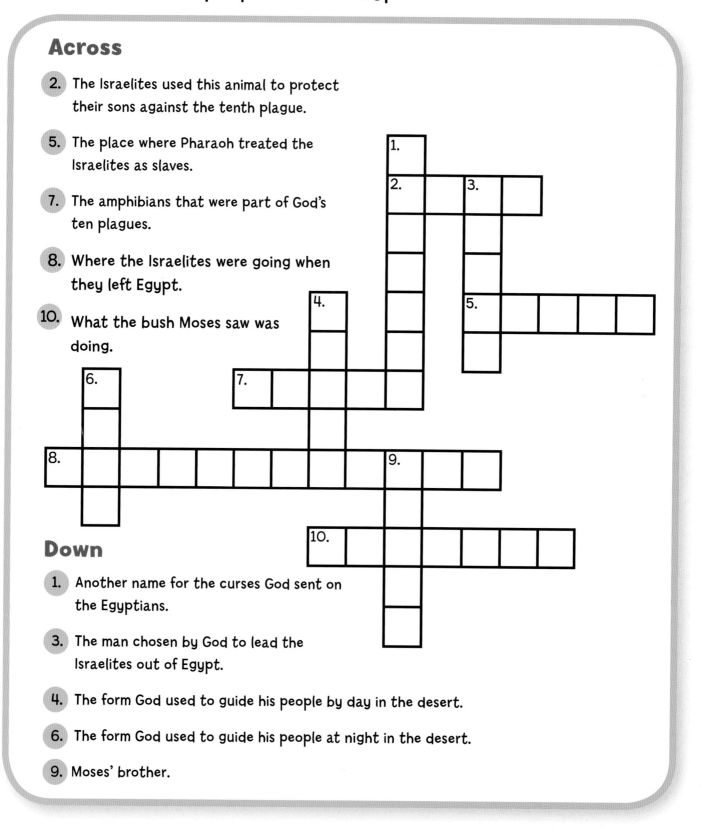

Down

1. Another name for the curses God sent on the Egyptians.

3. The man chosen by God to lead the Israelites out of Egypt.

4. The form God used to guide his people by day in the desert.

6. The form God used to guide his people at night in the desert.

9. Moses' brother.

In the story of the Good Samaritan, a man from Samaria stopped
to help someone in need when no one else would.
If you saw someone who needed help, what would you do?

Add yourself to the picture.

God created so many wonderful things! How many can you find?

Use the Word Bank below.

- ○ ANIMALS
- ○ BIRDS
- ○ DAY
- ○ FISH
- ○ LAND
- ○ MAN
- ○ MOON
- ○ OCEAN
- ○ PLANTS
- ○ SKY
- ○ STARS
- ○ SUN

```
M  N  S  O  L  E  Y  T  H  S  B  L
A  B  L  T  R  A  S  Y  L  Y  L  A
N  A  U  V  A  G  N  A  K  G  R  V
P  Y  A  P  T  R  M  D  A  X  G  D
B  M  B  N  W  I  S  T  S  N  A  W
S  I  A  D  N  K  L  S  K  Y  T  E
G  V  R  A  Q  G  D  N  R  D  U  S
X  G  N  D  M  O  O  N  O  F  E  U
G  O  O  R  S  Y  C  J  C  S  F  I
S  K  Y  M  L  D  R  V  E  R  I  S
G  P  L  A  N  T  S  F  A  F  S  Z
S  U  N  E  I  J  U  B  N  Y  H  C
```

Esther found the courage to speak to the king.

**Connect the dots to complete
the picture of brave Queen Esther.**

Jesus performed many miracles. Find the stickers that show his miracles in action.

Find and circle the five differences between these two pictures of Noah's ark.

Use the clues below to fill in the crossword puzzle.

Hint: read the story of Ruth and Naomi in Ruth 1-4.

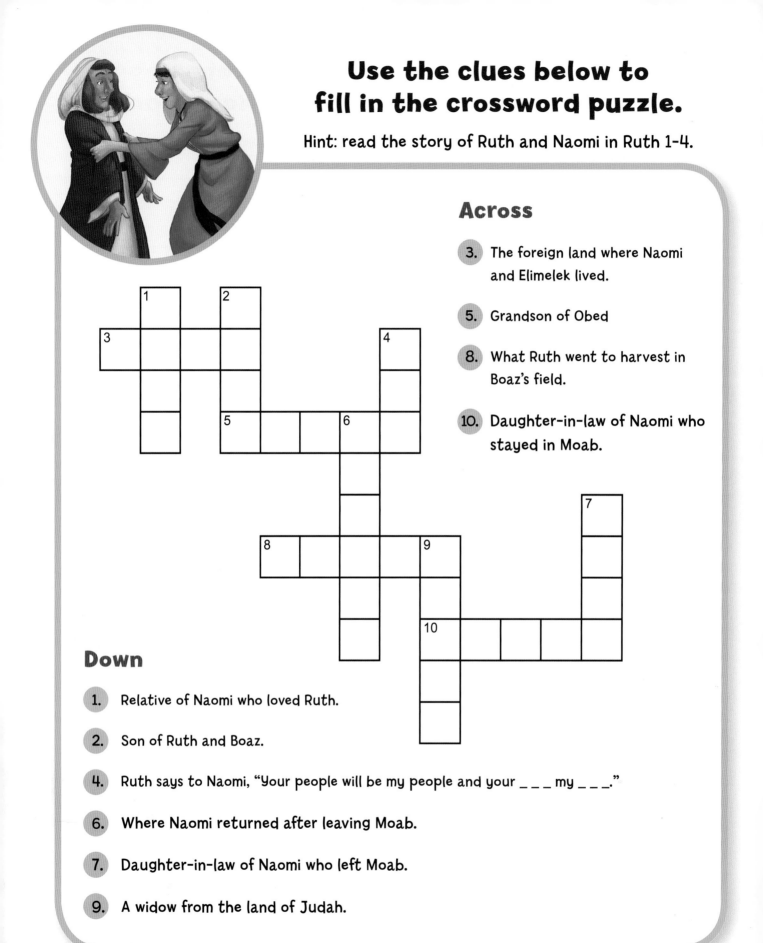

Across

3. The foreign land where Naomi and Elimelek lived.

5. Grandson of Obed

8. What Ruth went to harvest in Boaz's field.

10. Daughter-in-law of Naomi who stayed in Moab.

Down

1. Relative of Naomi who loved Ruth.

2. Son of Ruth and Boaz.

4. Ruth says to Naomi, "Your people will be my people and your _ _ _ my _ _ _."

6. Where Naomi returned after leaving Moab.

7. Daughter-in-law of Naomi who left Moab.

9. A widow from the land of Judah.

Moses and the Israelites had to find their way
out of Egypt, across the desert,
and through the waters of the Red Sea.

Help the Israelites find their way.

start

end

Word Scramble

Unscramble each of the clue words from the story of Queen Esther. Then take the letters that appear in ◯ boxes and unscramble them for the final message.

REESHT ☐☐◯☐☐☐

RACMOEDI ☐☐☐☐◯☐☐☐

EQNEU ☐☐◯☐☐

GIKN ☐☐☐☐

MAANH ◯☐☐☐☐

WEISHJ ◯☐◯☐◯☐

BRAVE QUEEN ESTHER SAVED ☐☐☐ ☐☐☐☐.

The Good Samaritan put differences with the Jews
behind him when he saved a hurt Jewish man.

Connect the dots to complete
the picture of the Good Samaritan.
Then color the picture.

Jesus once told people the story of a son who
left his family and went far away.
He wasted his money and then was homesick.
When the young man went home,
his father welcomed him back with a big hug.

Color this picture of a father's love.

Solve the secret code to find the hidden Bible verse said by Jesus.

,

___ _ __ _____;
23 6 7 8   15 22   17 19 26 17 9 23

____ _____.
21 14 10 8   15 22 5 9 22 11 22

A = 17	E = 22	I = 9	M = 16	Q = 12	U = 14	Y = 25
B = 15	F = 19	J = 21	N = 7	R = 26	V = 11	Z = 18
C = 1	G = 4	K = 2	O = 6	S = 10	W = 24	
D = 23	H = 13	L = 5	P = 3	T = 8	X = 20	

Answer: "Don't be afraid; just believe." Luke 8:50

20

Ruth and Naomi packed up everything they owned. They left Moab to return to Bethlehem.

Find and circle the five differences between these two pictures.

Noah Celebrates!

When Noah and his family left the ark, God put a rainbow in the sky. God promised never to flood the earth again.

Find the stickers to finish the picture of a celebration.

Find the five items that don't belong in the Garden of Eden. Put an X on them.

Find and circle words from the story of the Good Samaritan.

Use the Word Bank below.

○ GOOD   ○ LEVITE   ○ PRIEST   ○ ROBBER
○ HELP   ○ NEIGHBOR   ○ ROAD   ○ SAMARITAN

Q O Q L S Q S P G O O D K F D
S J U H W J L P L N H W F Y U
T E D Y F I L E V I T E M J D
S B Q H A S C T J J M T R J R
Y H E N B S Y Q V H P R O V U
N S T P J T T Q T B I J B M N
H E L P A T Z S E A D N B C A
D F C C H N G R Y I I M E K T
R Y P K Z N O S V K I M R M I
R O A D K B K G K E S O C P R
F A Y I H M E Q F L S B E Y A
K X E G R I A K N F H Y X B M
V L I P A D P R I E S T B H A
F E G W B V F V S I G D W Y S
N M S U R E X K J Q J X M W F

Use stickers to illustrate the story of the Lost Son.

1. A young boy leaves home.

2. He spends all his money.

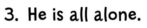

3. He is all alone.

4. He returns home to his family.

5. His father welcomes him back with open arms.

After Queen Esther saved her people,
everyone celebrated!

Find the 7 hidden items in this picture. Circle them.

Peacock

Chicken

Bowl of grapes

Sapphire ring

Three flags

Ruth met Boaz in a grain field.

Color in this picture of their first meeting.

Word Scramble

Unscramble each of the clue words from the story of Noah and the ark. Then take the letters that appear in ⬜ boxes and unscramble them for the final message.

HOAN

IARN

EDVO

BOTA

REWTA

GOD PUT A ⬜⬜⬜⬜⬜⬜⬜ IN THE SKY.

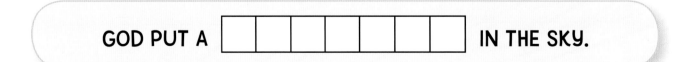